D1401772

Dream, Sparkle, CREATE

This book belongs to

What's your pony name?

Find out inside the book and write it here!

This edition published by Parragon Books Ltd in 2017 and distributed by

Parragon Inc.
440 Park Avenue South, 13th Floor
New York, NY 10016
www.parragon.com

Designed by Amy McHugh
Written and edited by Kayla Clibborn

HASBRO and its logo, MY LITTLE PONY and all related characters are trademarks of Hasbro and are used with permission. © 2017 Hasbro. All Rights Reserved.

All rights reserved. No part of this publication may be reproduced, stored in a retrieval system or transmitted, in any form or by any means, electronic, mechanical, photocopying, recording or otherwise, without the prior permission of the copyright holder.

ISBN 978-1-4748-9494-4

Printed in China

Pinkie Pie is **so excited** to see you!

Draw how Twilight Sparkle feels.

PaRragon

Bath · New York · Cologne · Melbourne · Delhi
Hong Kong · Shenzhen · Singapore

A cutie mark is the little picture on a pony's body. Ponies earn their marks when they discover their talent.

Design your own cutie mark here!

What's your special talent?

Write about it here.

Imagine you are a Pegasus like Rainbow Dash, and you have just learned to fly!

Where would you fly to first?

Write down three words to describe how flying feels.

How fast can you fly?

Color the power bars below to show your **speed.**

Sonic Rainboom!

Slow and **steady**

What can you see from above?

Draw the world far below you.

Pegasus wings come in all different **sizes,** colors, **and** patterns.

Design and color your own amazing set of wings.

Applejack is helping with the harvest at *Sweet Apple Acres.*

Fill the trees with delicious apples for her to pick.

Now that the harvest is complete, it's time to dream up a new apple-themed food for the Apple family to enjoy!

My food is called . . .

It tastes like . . .

You should eat it for . . .

Breakfast

Lunch

Dinner

Dessert

What does it look like? Draw it below!

It goes best with . . .

Sweetie Belle, Diamond Tiara, Lyra Heartstrings—the ponies of Equestria have amazing names.

What would your pony name be? Use the Key below to find out!

First letter of your first name:

A	ROSE
B	CINNAMON
C	SWEETIE
D	TWINKLE
E	SPARKLE
F	LILY
G	SHIMMER
H	CRYSTAL
I	GLIMMER
J	FAIRY
K	RAINBOW
L	JASMINE
M	GLITTER
N	LUNA
O	DIAMOND
P	FLITTER
Q	STARLIGHT
R	PRIMROSE
S	HONEY
T	CANDY
U	DAFFODIL
V	LILAC
W	PETAL
X	PEARL
Y	SUNSET
Z	SUGAR

First letter of your second name:

A	STAR
B	MAGIC
C	BELLE
D	DARLING
E	CHERRY
F	CUTIE
G	POSY
H	ROCKET
I	WISH
J	SHINE
K	DREAM
L	FLOWER
M	BLOSSOM
N	BERRY
O	BLOOM
P	CUPCAKE
Q	GLOW
R	FLUTTER
S	HEART
T	MEADOW
U	AURA
V	CLOUD
W	JEWEL
X	MOON
Y	DAISY
Z	GEM

My pony name is . . .

First: Last:

Now practice writing your pony name in cool and interesting ways.

Try bubble writing . . .

OR BLOCK WRITING . . .

or something fancy!

Twilight Sparkle writes a letter to Princess Celestia every week. Write your own letter to Celestia about anything you like. She can't wait to hear from you!

Don't forget to mail it!
Draw a postage stamp here:

Dear Princess Celestia,

With love from,

Write a letter to someone you love
and tell them something you've never told them before.

Dear,

With love from,

Now write a letter to someone you've never met!

Dear,

With love from,

Your imagination is an amazing thing! But even the most magical minds need a little help. These writing prompts have been sprinkled throughout the book for whenever you need a little boost of creativity.

Are you ready?

You've been whisked away on a cloud. Where do you end up?

Imagine your best friend is a giant, fire-breathing dragon. Describe your perfect day out together.

Let your imagination soar!

Rarity has designed an amazing new outfit. Give her a friendly compliment.

Pinkie Pie has invited you over for dinner. What's on the menu?

Equestria: A Magical History

MAGIC FOR BEGINNERS

Add titles to the books on her shelf.

Origins of the Elements of Harmony

CARING FOR YOUR DRAGON

Equestria is home to all sorts of **magical,** *mythical,*

Cockatrice is part chicken, part snake.

DISCORD IS PART PONY, PART DRAGON, PART EVERYTHING ELSE!

mixed-up creatures.

Draw some more crazy creatures like Cockatrice, Discord, and Gilda.

Gilda is part eagle, part lion!

★Uh-oh, **Sugarcube Corner has run out of treats!**

Fill the counter with delicious pastries and sweets to tempt the pony customers.

Invent a magical new dessert for Mrs. Cake to bake.

Name:

Ingredients:

Now draw it!

Add some of these ingredients for a little extra magic:

- ♥ a pinch of wanderlust
- ♥ a teaspoon of friendship
- ♥ a splash of adventure
- ♥ a dusting of sparkles

Zecora speaks in riddles and rhymes,
And now it's your turn to give it a try.
Just start with a word, like "cat", "sat", or "mat",
Then think to yourself, "what rhymes with that?"
Keep writing and rhyming and soon you will find
A poem has appeared from the depths of your mind.
Just use your creativity and go with the flow.

It's rhyme time.
Are you ready?

Get set...

Let's go!

Pinkie Pie represents the element of laughter.

Write down your funniest jokes to make her giggle.

Twilight Sparkle and her friends are always going on amazing adventures.

Dream up a **magical** new place for them to visit.

If you could live anywhere in Equestria, where would it be?

Why?

You're at your house in Ponyville when you hear a knock at the door.

Who's there?

Princess Celestia has given you an **important** task. What is it?

Your pet alligator has learned to talk! What's the first thing it says?

Write or draw . . . .

a thought in the bubble . . . . .

. . . a dream in the cloud . . . .

...a wish in the star...

...and something you love in the heart.

Celestia raises the sun each day. **Draw a beautiful sunrise.**

Luna brings out the moon at night. **Now draw the moon high** in the sky.

Fluttershy is a friend to all animals.

Fill the butterfly wings with different patterns and colors.

Imagine you are lost in the **dark** and **gloomy** Everfree Forest. **What can you ...**

... see?

... hear?

... smell?

... feel?

Twilight sees the magic

Use your imagination to turn these shapes into wonderful things.

Tell Twilight Sparkle about your favorite book.

Applejack has asked you to help out at Sweet Apple Acres. Describe your day.

You are a pony from Canterlot visiting Cloudsdale. Report back to your hometown about your visit.

Princess Luna has asked for your help to raise the moon. How do you do it?

Imagine this page is the sky and fill it with clouds for Rainbow Dash to clear.

Try drawing tiny, fluffy clouds.

Now draw a big, gray storm cloud.

Rarity
needs some
fashion inspiration
for her next outfit.
Fill these pages
with perfect
patterns
like

... stripes ...

polka dots or ... zigzags?

Imagine you are a Unicorn with a magical horn, just like **Rarity.**

Would you use your magic for:

Good?

Bad?

A little of both?

What's the first thing you'd do with your magic powers?

What does your *magic* look like? Draw it below.

Spike just **l♥ves** eating jewels and gems!

Fill this page with sparkly treats of different shapes, sizes, and colors.

Imagine you have a magical sidekick.

What kind of creature would it be, and what would it eat?

Draw your sidekick enjoying its favorite snack.

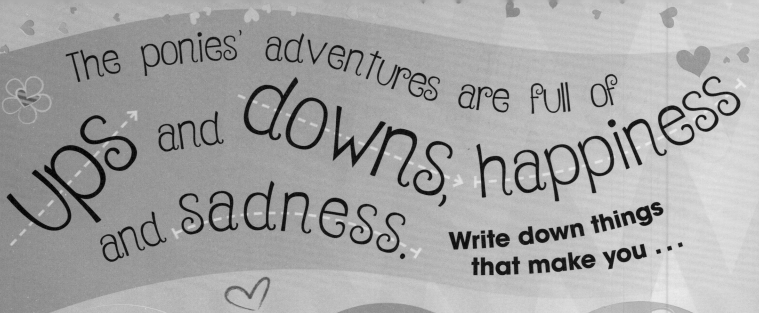

The ponies' adventures are full of **ups** and **downs, happiness and sadness.**

Write down things that make you . . .

Excited

Angry

Sleepy

Sad

Happy

Can you think of a different emotion?

Draw it on the pony face, and then write about how it makes you feel.

You find Fluttershy sitting alone looking sad. What do you do to cheer her up?

Imagine you are a pony villain like Queen Chrysalis. Write your to-do list for today.

You suddenly become a huge celebrity like Sapphire Shores. Practice signing your autograph for your fans.

Imagine your pen is a magic wand. Write a spell without taking your pen off the page.

Uh-oh,
the Weather Factory
in Cloudsdale has
broken!

Fill these pages with **snowflakes**, **raindrops**, **sunbeams**, **rainbows**, and **any other weather** you can think of.

Pinkie Pie just *loves* to perform!

Write a new song for Pinkie
to sing to her friends.

Twilight once accidentally cast a spell on her pony pals, swapping their talents and destinies! Imagine you could swap lives with anyone, or anypony. . . .

Who would you choose?

Why?

What's the first thing you'd do?

Where's the first place you'd go?

What about the person (or pony) that you swapped lives with?

Describe their day in your life.

Friendship is magic!

You can never have too many friends.
Dream up a new pony pal to join Twilight,
Pinkie Pie, Rarity, and their friends.

Name:

Talent:

Cutie mark:

They love . . .

They hate . . .

Describe this pony in one word: